DATE OF RETURN

WATERSIDE

27/11/??

0 6 APR 2005

19. DEC. 2001

17. DEC 2002

6 JUN 2005

29. DEC. 2003

3 JAN 2008

13. JAN ??

23 DEC 2009

- 4 JAN 2012

2 MAR 2005

2 9 DEC 2012

D1419853

Text copyright © Chris Powling 1999
Illustrations copyright © David Mostyn 1999

First published in Great Britain in 1999
by Macdonald Young Books
an imprint of Wayland Publishers Ltd
61 Western Road
Hove
East Sussex
BN3 1JD

Find Macdonald Young Books on the internet at
http://www.myb.co.uk

The right of Chris Powling to be identified as the author
and David Mostyn the illustrator of this Work has been
asserted by them in accordance with the
Copyright, Designs and Patents Act 1988

Designed and Typeset by Danny McBride
Printed in Hong Kong by Wing King Tong

British Library Cataloguing in Publication Data available

ISBN: 0 7500 2880 7

CHRIS POWLING

Long John Santa

Illustrated by David Mostyn

MACDONALD YOUNG BOOKS

Chapter One

Long John the pirate had an ache in his
bones and a crick in his neck. "Am I too old
to be a buccaneer?" he wondered. "All the
wind and the wet is destroyin' me 'ealth,
I reckon. There must be an easier way to
make a livin'..."

So he went ashore to find out.

The man at the Job Centre wasn't impressed. He clucked his tongue and looked over his glasses, disapprovingly. "Have you got any skills?" he asked. "Or tools, maybe?"

"Tools?" said Long John.

"Yes, tools – you know, the sort of thing a handyman has."

Long John stroked his beard. "Well, there's this 'ere cutlass I always carries – and this pair o' pistols I wears in me belt. Remarkable 'andy, they are."

"How about exams, then?"

"Exams, matey? Now I'm glad you asked me that. I can examine a treasure map like a good 'un, or a sail comin' over the 'orizon. Is that what you're after?"

"Not quite," sniffed the Job Centre man. "What sort of money had you in mind?"

"Doubloons would suit me fine, son. Either those or pieces-of-eight."

And Long John spat politely into a convenient waste-paper bin.

This almost finished the interview. "Look," said the man at the Job Centre, "can you come back after Christmas? At the moment I've only got one vacancy on offer. But it means working with children, you see—"

"Children?" growled Long John. "That's fine by me, young feller-me-lad. As it 'appens, I'm very partial to children. Toasted, for preference..."

"I'm sorry, sir. I really don't think…"

"Then think again, matey."

The Job Centre man couldn't help agreeing with him instantly.

"There," said Long John as he lowered his cutlass and tucked the pistol back in his belt. "I told you 'ow 'andy they are."

Chapter Two

Long John's cutlass and pistol were handy later on as well. This was when Long John talked to the manager of the Toy Department in the biggest and poshest shop in town. She took a hasty step backwards, smiling as brightly as she could.

"Of course you can have the job," she squeaked. "After all, you've already got a red coat and a white beard!"

"Thank'ee, kindly," said Long John. "I knew you'd see it my way. Folks normally do."

This time, just as politely, he spat into a potted plant.

Of course, the customers were a bit surprised at first. It was rather unusual to see the skull and crossbones flying over Father Christmas' grotto – especially in the biggest and poshest shop in town.

Luckily, Long John helped the customers to see it his way.

"I'm a seafaring Santa," he explained to them at gun point, "with a wooden leg."

"Really?" people said nervously.

"You bet I am. That's why I've got a picture of a mermaid tattoo'd all over me tum. She's sunbathin' under a bunch of mistletoe.

Want a quick peek?"

"Er... no, thanks. Not just now."

"Please yourself, mateys."

And he gave them a horrible wink with his glinty, sea-green eye – the one not covered by a black patch, that is.

Chapter Three

Long John got the hang of his new job very quickly. Or so it seemed to him. One early visitor was a snooty-looking lad dressed in the latest designer clothes.

"Now then, me 'andsome," said the pirate. "What's your fancy for Christmas mornin'?"

"Listen carefully," the boy snapped, "and then maybe this year you won't make any mistakes. I want a personalized laptop computer, a personalized mobile videophone, a personalized laser-gun with telescopic sights and a personalized three-dimensional electronic chess set."

"Personalized, eh?" Long John nodded.

"Every item designed for me personally, yes. And that's only for starters. What I also want is… is…"

His words trailed away.

Polite as ever, the old pirate spat over his own shoulder straight into the lucky dip.

After this, he bent forward on his chair until his chin was so close to the boy's it was hard to see which one of them owned the beard.

"OK, matey," said Long John, "that's what you *want*, no sweat. 'Ere's what you're goin' to *get*, though… assumin' I've got anythin' to do with it."

He dropped his voice to a whisper.

No one else ever found out what he said, exactly. But it was so personalized, the snooty-looking lad dressed in the latest designer clothes ran screaming all the way home.

Chapter Four

There were other incidents, too. Marooning
was mentioned more than once and so
was keelhauling, being clapped in irons
and walking the plank. To be fair, this only
happened to some kids. For others, the ones
who were "too good to be toasted" in Long
John's opinion, there was a promise of calm
seas, fresh breezes and maybe – just maybe –
buried treasure.

Naturally, some people complained –
particularly about the spitting. "Only a few,
though," said the manager of the Toy
Department, happily, as she counted the
people in the queue.

This stretched away from the grotto, down
the stairs, out of the main entrance and
along the pavement in front of all the other
big, posh shops in the High Street.

"Oh dear," she smiled. "We seem to be
luring away most of their customers..."

This was true.

What's more, the new seafaring Santa with a wooden leg was attracting publicity as well. Before long, reports appeared in the newspapers, followed by interviews on radio and television. That's when the first of the letters arrived:

Dear Father Pirate

I've been really good this year. So will you please bring me a cutlass, and a pair of flintlock pistols, just like yours, on Christmas night? They'll be very handy, I think.

Oh, and will you let me have a quick look under your eyepatch if I'm still awake? I'll leave you a glass of grog and a ship's biscuit under the Christmas tree. Love from your friend,

Joanna (aged 7)

Long John read it over and over again. "I've never had fan mail before!" he beamed.

More letters came with the next post. And even more with the post after that... not to mention the ones after *that*. Soon, a couple of sackfuls a day were arriving by special delivery.

Chapter Five

On Christmas Eve, when everyone else at
the biggest and poshest shop in town had
gone home to bed, Long John was still
opening envelopes.

"I just can't fathom it," he groaned.
"There's enough paper 'ere to capsize a
man o' war. I'll be stuck in this berth for
ever at this rate."

"Serves you right," came a voice as deep and rumbly as his own.

Long John looked up in surprise.

Peering into the grotto was someone red-coated, white-bearded and much the same size as himself – except with an extra leg and an extra eye. Judging by the scowl on his face, there was no chance at all he'd see things Long John's way.

"Call yourself a helper?" he growled. "Help like yours I can do without!"

" 'Old on, matey. You must be—"

"According to most people, I'm Father Christmas – the genuine, one and only, land, sea and airfaring Santa with a wooden sleigh. At least, that's who I was until recently. Now, I'm not so sure."

" 'Ow's that then?"

"Because of you, that's how. Year in and year out I've clambered up and down chimneys along with rooting round radiators and suchlike.

Believe me, that underfloor central heating is a killer. And what thanks do I get? All of a sudden, some moth-eaten old sea dog makes a take-over bid without so much as a by your leave and – bless me! – he becomes a star overnight!"

Long John shifted uncomfortably in his chair. "Er... I can see why you're feelin' a bit low in the water," he admitted. "A bit low in the water? That's not the half of it, you maritime monstrosity. It's enough to make me spit."

Which Father Christmas nearly did until he remembered this was Long John's speciality.

The old pirate scratched thoughtfully at one of his scars. "Listen, matey," he frowned. "I weren't makin' 'eavy weather for you on purpose. This star stuff 'appened by accident. D'you think I want to spend me life squintin' through a pile of post? It's worse than bein' adrift in the Doldrums.

Speakin' for myself, I'd rather earn a livin' scrapin' barnacles off a battleship's bum."

"Is that true?" said Father suspiciously.

"Cross me 'eart and 'ope to d̲. not yet awhile for preference. Why, ̲ weren't for this crick in me neck and t̲ bones achin' like billy-o, I'd still be cruisin the Spanish Main."

"In that case…"

ather Christmas took a deep breath to
lm himself down. "In that case, we can
move to Plan B," he said.

"Plan B, matey?"

"Follow me, I've set everything up below."

Chapter Six

Still muttering about helpers who were more of a hindrance, Santa led the way downstairs to the Sports and Leisure Department.

This was as splendid as you'd expect in the biggest and poshest shop in town.

What, almost certainly, you wouldn't have expected was the strange-looking object on the main display stand.

"There," Father Christmas pointed. "Essential equipment for Plan B. What do you think?"

Long John lifted an eyebrow. "Well, matey," he said, "if that's a ship, I'd abandon it."

"Of course it isn't a ship – not exactly, anyway. It's my second-best sleigh. I've had it personalized. No reindeer, for instance. As you can see, it's wind-powered with wheels for land travel and a rudder for seafaring. It'll even fly short distances if you catch the right gust under these wings."

"All very 'andy, I'm sure," said Long John. "But where do I come in?"

Father Christmas tugged at a rope.

From the topmost mast of his personalized, second-best sleigh, fluttered a crisp, new skull and crossbones.

It was a tricky moment.

The old sea dog fingered his cutlass. "So now you want my job, matey. Is that 'ow the wind is blowin'?"

"Certainly not, you nautical nitwit. This sleigh has been personalized for *you*. Plan B is for you to help me with some of my deliveries – it's the least you can do after all the trouble you've caused. On a night as dark as this people will never notice which of us has paid them a visit. Who knows, I might even finish early for once. Is it a deal?"

"Worth considerin'," Long John shrugged.

"Any chance of a doubloon or two by way of wages? Or a few pieces of eight?"

"Wages?" choked Father Christmas.

He dropped his voice to a whisper.

No one else ever found out exactly what he said. Let's just say it involved Plan A and was as personalized as his second-best sleigh. Anyone except a pirate would have run screaming all the way out of the shop.

Even Long John himself didn't argue. "OK, me 'andsome," he grumbled. " 'Ave it your way, then."

"I will," said Father Christmas.

And he did.

Chapter Seven

So, a little later, when all the kids in the world were safely asleep, Long John the pirate set sail again.

Here and there, admittedly, Christmas morning brought a bit of a surprise. "Hey, look at our Christmas tree," a small girl exclaimed. "The fairy lights are spelling out a message... they say YO-HO-HO!"

"How come there's a
ship in this empty bottle?"
someone's dad wanted to
know. "Last night it was
full of the finest rum!"

"Oh, dear," a big sister
giggled. "Granny must
have stuck her nose in
once too often."

Mostly, though,
wherever he went
aboard – from a
fisherman's cottage to
a cross-channel ferry –
Long John was on his
best behaviour. No one
spotted him, either,
apart from Joanna
(aged 7) who promised
she wouldn't tell a soul.

By the time the sun came up, the old pirate was exhausted. "Not only that but me neck and bones are as bad as ever," he complained. "It's 'cos I'm back in the wind and the wet, I reckon."

Suddenly, in a corner of the sleigh, something caught his eye.

It was small, mysterious and wrapped up in Christmas paper as neatly as a folded flag.

Long John stared at it, gloomily. " 'Ave I forgotten to deliver the last present?" he groaned. "No, 'ang on a tick. Isn't that my name on the label?"

It was.

There was a note as well:

Dear Long John

I know all about the cricks and aches – what with chimneys, radiators and underfloor central heating to cope with. Here's the ointment I use to get rid of them. I've never known it fail.

Love from
The Real Santa

PS. The ointment's been personalized, of course. So kindly keep off my patch next Christmas.

Already Long John felt better.

As he sat back in the second-best sleigh, with its sails and wheels and wings, there was a wicked glint in the old sea dog's eye – the one not covered by a black patch, that is.

"Christmas, matey?" he chuckled. "That's fine as far as it goes. But why stick to Christmas? A vessel like this strikes me as remarkable 'andy all the year round!"

Long John the pirate was back in business.

Look out for more titles in the Super Stars range:

Superheroes Down the Plughole by Keith Brumpton
Elasticman, Mothgirl and the others have lost their powers...
When they learn that the Superhero Inspectorate is coming to
check them out, the pressure is on. Can our clapped-out crew
of caped crusaders prove once and for all that they really are
still superheroes?!

Make 'em Laugh by Clare Bevan
Charley Muddle's got the red nose, the baggy trousers and the
revolving tie. He's all set to be a brilliant clown. The trouble is,
Charley's heart just isn't in it. From his first day at clown school,
he can't seem to do a thing wrong! Does Charley have what it
takes to make 'em laugh?

You can buy all these books from your local bookseller, or they
can be ordered direct from the publisher. For more information
about Super Stars, write to: *The Sales Department, Macdonald Young
Books, 61 Western Road, Hove, East Sussex BN3 1JD.*